This
Treasure Cove Story
belongs to

KAMSI

MARY POPPINS

A CENTUM BOOK 978-1-912396-72-6
Published in Great Britain by Centum Books Ltd.
This edition published 2018.

3 5 7 9 10 8 6 4 2

Centum Books Ltd, 20 Devon Square, Newton Abbot,
Devon, TQ12 2HR, UK.

www.centumbooksltd.co.uk | books@centumbooksltd.co.uk
CENTUM BOOKS Limited Reg.No. 07641486.

A CIP catalogue record for this book is available
from the British Library.

Printed in China.

centum

WALT DISNEY'S
Mary Poppins

Adapted by Annie North Bedford
Based on the Walt Disney Motion Picture
Illustrated by Al White

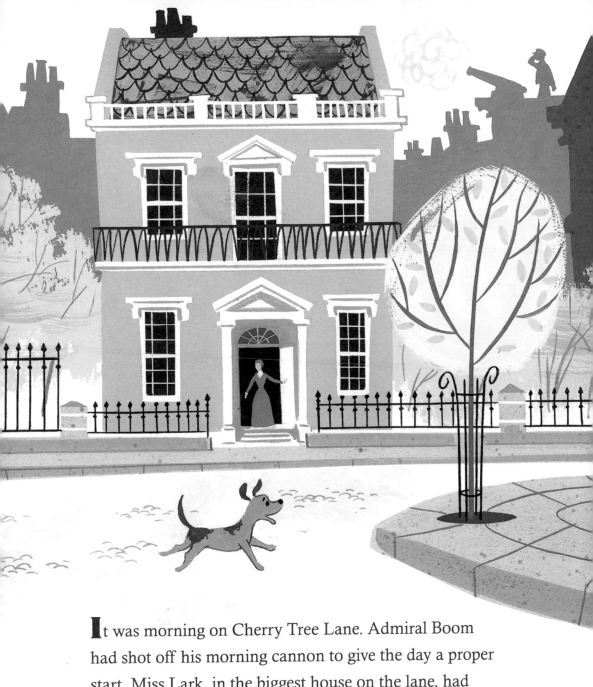

It was morning on Cherry Tree Lane. Admiral Boom
had shot off his morning cannon to give the day a proper
start. Miss Lark, in the biggest house on the lane, had
sent her dog, Andrew, out for his morning stroll.

But in the nursery at number 17 Cherry Tree Lane,
Jane and Michael Banks were still in bed.

'Up, up!' said Mary Poppins, their nanny, pulling back
the blankets with a firm hand. 'We'll have no lounging
about on a super-cali-fragi-listic-expi-ali-do-cious day.'

'Super-cali-what, Mary Poppins?' asked Michael.

'Close your mouth, Michael. We are not a codfish. Super-cali-fragi-listic-expi-ali-do-cious, of course. If you can't think of a word that says just what you want to say, try super-cali-fragi-listic-expi-ali-do-cious. And it *just* describes today.'

That got Jane and Michael up and dressed and breakfasted in record time.

'Out to the park we go,' said Mary Poppins, hurrying them into their hats and coats. 'Spit-spot, this way.'

'Super-cali-fragi-listic-expi-ali-do-cious!' sang Jane and Michael as they marched along the lane. They almost bumped into Mary Poppins when she stopped to speak to Andrew, Miss Lark's little dog.

'Yip yap yap,' said Andrew.

'Slower, please,' said Mary Poppins. 'I can't understand a word you say.'

'Yip yap yap,' said Andrew, slower.

'Again?' said Mary Poppins.

'Yap yap,' said Andrew.

'Yes, of course,' said Mary Poppins.
'I'll go straightaway. And thank you very much.'
    'Yap,' said Andrew.
    Then, taking Jane and Michael by the hand,
Mary Poppins started off the way Andrew had come.
    'What did he say?' asked Jane.
    'He said, *you're welcome*,' said Mary Poppins.
    'But what else did he say?' Jane insisted.

'I don't think he said anything at all,'
said Michael crossly. 'And I thought we were
going for a walk in the park.'

'There's been a change of plans,' said Mary
Poppins. 'Come along, please. Don't straggle.'

She led them at a brisk pace down narrow, twisting
streets they had never seen before. Then she stopped
at the door of a small house.

Rap, rap went the parrot's-head handle of Mary Poppins'
umbrella. The door was opened by Mary's friend Bert.

'How is he?' Mary Poppins asked. Bert shook his head.
'Never seen him like this,' he said. 'And that's the truth.'
Mary Poppins led Jane and Michael inside the house.
They found themselves in a large, cheerful room.
In the centre stood a table set for tea.

'Bless my soul,' gurgled a voice rich with chuckles. 'Is that Mary Poppins? I'm delighted to see you, my dear.'

Jane and Michael looked about. They could see no one else in the room.

'Uncle Albert, you promised not to go floating around again!' she said. And she seemed to be speaking to the ceiling.

Jane and Michael looked up. There in the air sat Mary Poppins' uncle Albert, chuckling merrily.

'I know, my dear,' said Uncle Albert, wiping
a merry eye. 'I tried – really, I did. But I do so enjoy
laughing, you know.' Here the chuckles bubbled up
so that he bobbed against the ceiling. 'And the moment
I start – *hee, hee* – it's all *up* with me.' To the children
he whispered, 'It's laughing that does it, you know.'

Jane and Michael were trying hard to be polite. They
kept their faces straight. But first the laughter sparkled out
of their eyes. Then it bubbled up their throats. They began
to chuckle.

By this time Bert was rolling about, shaking with laughter. As they watched, he rose into the air and soon was bobbing about beside Uncle Albert.

Michael's chuckle grew to a laugh. So did Jane's. Soon they were simply filled with laughter. It bubbled out and they felt lighter and lighter until their feet left the floor and they floated up to the ceiling!

'How nice,' said Uncle Albert. 'I was hoping you'd turn up. Do make yourselves comfortable, my dears.'

'I must say you're a sight, the lot of you,' said Mary Poppins, her arms folded in a way that Jane and Michael knew meant she disapproved.

'You know, speaking of sights,' said Bert, 'that reminds me of my brother who has a nice cushy job in a watch factory.'

'Is that so?' said Uncle Albert. 'What does he do?'

'You know what he does!' gasped Bert, who was laughing so hard he could scarcely speak. 'He stands around in this watch factory all day and *makes faces.*'

At that, all four of them roared so with laughter that they turned somersaults in the air.

'I found a horseshoe today,'
said Bert, holding his sides.
'You know what that means?'

'I certainly do,' said Uncle
Albert. 'It means that some
poor horse is walking around
in his stocking feet.'

Again the room rocked with
laughter. Only Mary Poppins
looked stern.

'Most disgraceful thing
I've ever seen,' she snapped,
'or my name isn't Mary Poppins.'

'Speaking of names,' said Bert, 'I know a man with a wooden leg named Smith…'

'Really?' chortled Uncle Albert. 'What's the name of his other leg?'

More gusts of laughter.

'Now then, Jane, Michael! It is time for tea,' said Mary Poppins firmly from below. 'I will not have my schedule disrupted.'

'Oh, please stay!' begged Uncle Albert. He pointed
at the table on the floor. 'I have a splendid tea waiting
for us – if you could, er, manage to get the table to…'

With a rattle and a bump, the table began to jerk. Then
up it rose through the air – cups, cakes, teapot and all.

'Oh, splendid, splendid! Thank you, my dear,' said
Uncle Albert. Then, to Michael and Jane, 'Keep your feet
back, my dears. Watch the cups and mind the jam.'

'Next thing, I suppose you'll be wanting me to pour,'
said Mary Poppins with a sigh. And up she floated, neat
as you please, without so much as a smile.

The others still laughed and bobbled about as Mary Poppins poured and passed the tea – with milk for Michael and Jane.

'Thank you, my dear,' said Uncle Albert. 'I'm having such a good time. I wish you could all stay up here with me always.'

'We'll jolly well have to.' Michael grinned. 'There's no way to get down.'

'Well, to be honest,' said Uncle Albert, 'there *is* a way. Just think of something sad and down you go.'

But who could think of anything sad? They chuckled at the very idea.

'Time to go home!' Mary Poppins' voice, crisp and firm, cut sharply through the laughter.

And suddenly, at that sad thought, down came Jane and Michael, Uncle Albert and Bert, *bump, bump, bump, bump* on the floor.

'Goodbye,' said Michael. 'We'll be back soon.'

'And thank you,' said Jane soberly. 'We've had a lovely time.'

'Oh, dear.' Uncle Albert was sobbing as he waved goodbye. 'It makes me so sad to see them leave.'

Back home, Jane and Michael tried to tell their father about their adventure.

'We floated in the air and had tea on the ceiling,' Jane began.

'And there was this man with a wooden leg named Smith,' Michael broke in.

'Poppins!' cried Mr. Banks. 'What is the meaning of this?'

'Children will be children,' sniffed Mary Poppins. 'And these two are up past their bedtime. Spit-spot.' And she marched them off to the nursery, muttering, 'The very idea!'

Michael and Jane just looked at each other.

'Anyway,' said Jane, kicking off a slipper, 'it was a super-cali-fragi-listic-expi-ali-do-cious day!'

Treasure Cove Stories

•Book list may be subject to change.